Published in 1991 by G. P. Putnam's Sons, a division of
The Putnam and Grosset Book Group, 200 Madison Avenue,
New York, NY 10016

Originally published in 1990 in Great Britain by Piccadilly
Press Ltd. London

Published simultaneously in Canada

Printed in Hong Kong by South China Printing Co. (1988) Ltd.
Designed by COOPER WILSON
Typeset by The Text Unit, London EC1

Library of Congress Cataloging-in-Publication Data
West, Keith, Little Pig's Special Day/Keith West. –
1st American ed p. cm.
Summary: Little Pig is very excited on a very special day,
when something new and wonderful is going to happen.
[1. Pig's – Fiction. 2. Babies – Fiction.] I. Title.
PZ7. W5184LI 1991 [E] – dc20 89-78377 CIP AC
ISBN 0-399-22209-X

1   3   5   7   9   10   8   6   4   2

First American edition

KEITH WEST

Little Pig's Special Day

G. P. PUTNAM'S SONS • NEW YORK

Little Pig wakes up. He is excited — today is a *special* day.

Dad says, "Time for breakfast, Little Pig. Quickly now!"

Little Pig sits down for breakfast.
He feels fizzy — this is a *special* day.

"There's milk and porridge and toast and honey. Eat up, Little Pig."

But the porridge is lumpy — not like Mom's porridge.
The toast is black — not like Mom's toast.
Little Pig is disappointed.

Then Little Pig smiles. He remembers that today is a *special* day.
He says, "Dad, I can't eat — I feel fizzy."

Little Pig helps do the dishes,
take out the garbage,
and make the beds.

He helps mop the floors,
cleans the bathtub,
and puts away his toys.
Everything is clean and tidy for this *special* day.

Dad takes Little Pig to stay with Mrs. Jones.
Then he goes into town.

Mrs. Jones pours lemonade and brings out ginger cookies.

Little Pig drinks the lemonade but he says,
"I don't think I want a cookie today, thank you.
I can't eat because I feel fizzy."

"Ah yes, Little Pig, I understand," says Mrs. Jones. "Today is a *special* day. You can eat something later."

Then she takes Little Pig outside.

He visits the chickens and finds an egg.
They bring in the washing,

feed the goldfish,
and take letters
to the mailbox.

"Just look at the time," says Mrs. Jones. "We have to get back to your house. I promised that I would light a fire to make the living room cozy."

They hurry up the lane.

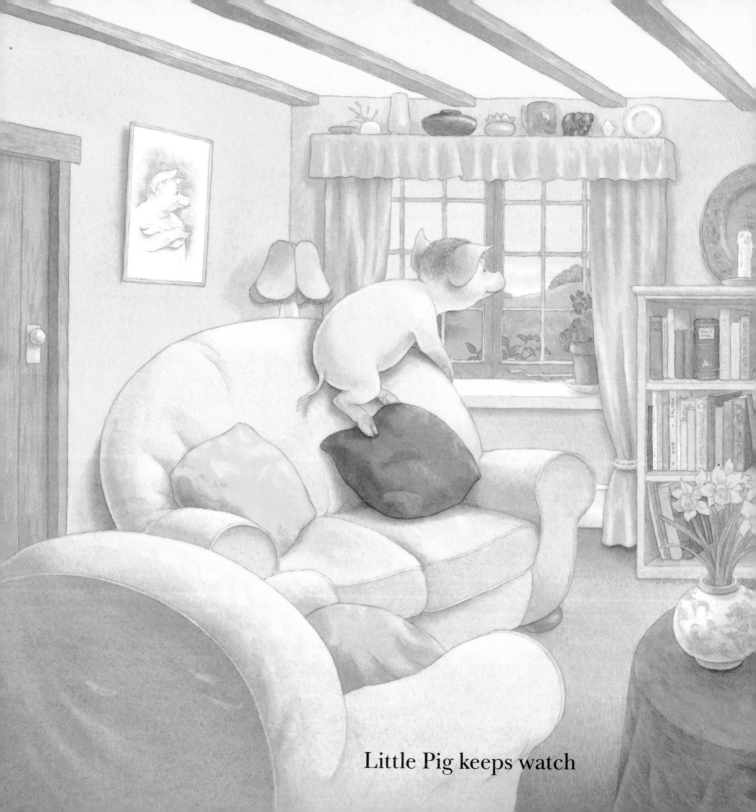

Little Pig keeps watch

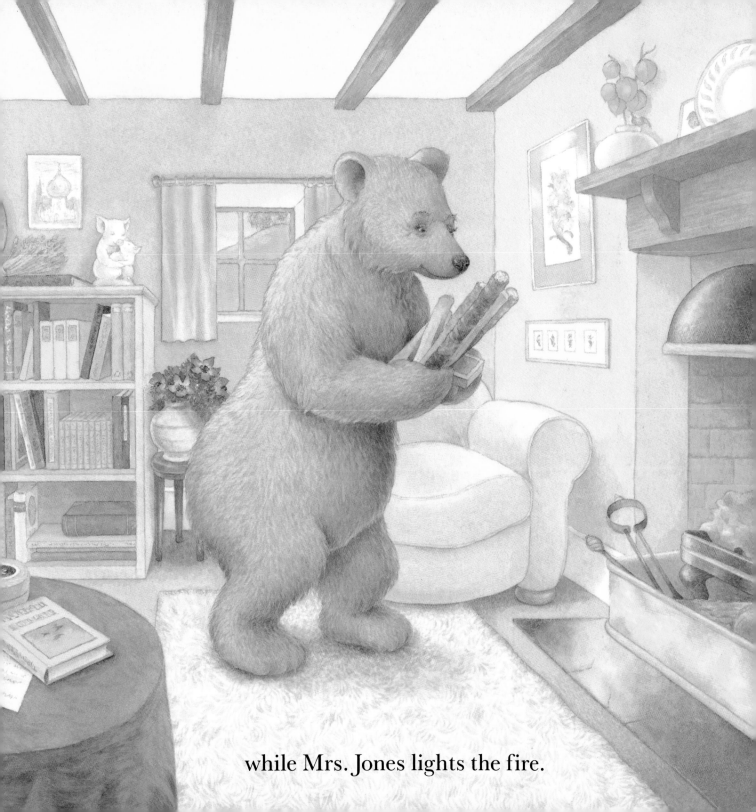

while Mrs. Jones lights the fire.

Little Pig runs to the door.
Here is Dad and here is Mom *and here is a new Baby Piglet!*

"This is a *special, special* day," cries Little Pig.

Mom says, "Please stay for coffee and cake, Mrs. Jones."
"Would Piglet like something to eat?" says Little Pig.
"Now *I am* hungry."